Go Ducks!™

Aimee Aryal

Illustrated by Rafael D. Nazario

It was a beautiful fall day at the University of Oregon. Oregon fans were on their way to Autzen Stadium for a Ducks game.

One Duck family was strolling
through campus. At Johnson Hall,
the family was greeted by Oregon
fans cheering, "Go Ducks!"

The family walked to Erb Memorial
Union, where they cheered with other
Duck fans at a pep rally.

Everyone was excited for the football game. Oregon fans shouted, "Go Ducks!"

The family walked over to
historic Deady Hall, the oldest
building on campus.

The Pioneer statue was the family's next stop. A friendly couple waved and said, "Go Ducks!"

At the Duck Store, the family picked
up Oregon clothing and souvenirs.

After finding their favorite Oregon gear,
the family was ready for the game!
They yelled, "Go Ducks!"

Their next stop was Memorial Quad
for a picnic. The family enjoyed a
great lunch and the beautiful weather.

Nearby, students were playing on the Quad. The students chanted, "Go Ducks!"

Outside Knight Library, the family ran
into a librarian heading to work.

The librarian was happy to see so
many Oregon fans on campus.
She called out, "Go Ducks!"

In front of McArthur Court, the
family ran into a group of
Oregon Alumni. The alumni
hollered, "Go Ducks!"

Outside the Student Rec Center, more
Oregon fans gathered for the big game.
Fans cheered, "Go Ducks!"

Finally, the family arrived at
Autzen Stadium – home of the
University of Oregon Ducks.

As fans crossed the Autzen footbridge,
they roared, "Go Ducks!"

The family watched the game from the stands with thousands of other Duck fans. The Ducks scored!

After scoring a touchdown, the quarterback looked into the stands and called, "Go Ducks!"

At halftime, the University of Oregon Marching Band ran on to the field and marched into formation.

The band played *Mighty Oregon* as fans shouted, "Win, Ducks, win!"

The University of Oregon Ducks
won the football game! Players and
coaches celebrated the victory.

The players gave the coach an unexpected shower! The coach cheered, "Go Ducks!"

After the game, the family headed home. It had been a fun day at the University of Oregon.

Back home, the children were soon fast asleep and dreaming about the next Oregon football game.

Go Ducks!

For Anna and Maya. ~ Aimee Aryal

For my parents Margarita and Rafael, Sr. - Rafael D. Nazario

For more information about our products,
please visit us online at www.mascotbooks.com.

For more information, please contact Mascot Books,
P.O. Box 220157, Chantilly, VA 20153-0157

PRT0910C

ISBN: 1-934878-19-7

Printed in the United States.

Title List

Baseball

Boston Red Sox	Hello, Wally!	Jerry Remy
Boston Red Sox	Wally And His Journey Through Red Sox Nation!	Jerry Remy
Boston Red Sox	Coast to Coast with Wally	Jerry Remy
Boston Red Sox	A Season with Wally	Jerry Remy
Colorado Rockies	Hello, Dinger!	Aimee Aryal
Detroit Tigers	Hello, Paws!	Aimee Aryal
New York Yankees	Let's Go, Yankees!	Yogi Berra
New York Yankees	Yankees Town	Aimee Aryal
New York Mets	Hello, Mr. Met!	Rusty Staub
New York Mets	Mr. Met and his Journey Through the Big Apple	Aimee Aryal
St. Louis Cardinals	Hello, Fredbird!	Ozzie Smith
Philadelphia Phillies	Hello, Phillie Phanatic!	Aimee Aryal
Chicago Cubs	Let's Go, Cubs!	Aimee Aryal
Chicago White Sox	Let's Go, White Sox!	Aimee Aryal
Cleveland Indians	Hello, Slider!	Bob Feller
Seattle Mariners	Hello, Mariner Moose!	Aimee Aryal
Washington Nationals	Hello, Screech!	Aimee Aryal
Milwaukee Brewers	Hello Bernie Brewer!	Aimee Aryal

College

Alabama	Hello, Big Al!	Aimee Aryal
Alabama	Roll Tide!	Ken Stabler
Alabama	Big Al's Journey Through the Yellowhammer State	Aimee Aryal
Arizona	Hello, Wilbur!	Lute Olson
Arkansas	Hello, Big Red!	Aimee Aryal
Arkansas	Big Red's Journey Through the Razorback State	Aimee Aryal
Auburn	Hello, Aubie!	Aimee Aryal
Auburn	War Eagle!	Pat Dye
Auburn	Aubie's Journey Through the Yellowhammer State	Aimee Aryal
Boston College	Hello, Baldwin!	Aimee Aryal
Brigham Young	Hello, Cosmo!	LaVell Edwards
Cal - Berkeley	Hello, Oski!	Aimee Aryal
Clemson	Hello, Tiger!	Aimee Aryal
Clemson	Tiger's Journey Through the Palmetto State	Aimee Aryal
Colorado	Hello, Ralphie!	Aimee Aryal
Connecticut	Hello, Jonathan!	Aimee Aryal
Duke	Hello, Blue Devil!	Aimee Aryal
Florida	Hello, Albert!	Aimee Aryal
Florida	Albert's Journey Through the Sunshine State	Aimee Aryal
Florida State	Let's Go, 'Noles!	Aimee Aryal
Georgia	Hello, Hairy Dawg!	Aimee Aryal
Georgia	How 'Bout Them Dawgs!	Vince Dooley
Georgia	Hairy Dawg's Journey Through the Peach State	Vince Dooley
Georgia Tech	Hello, Buzz!	Aimee Aryal
Gonzaga	Spike, The Gonzaga Bulldog	Mike Pringle
Illinois	Let's Go, Illini!	Aimee Aryal
Indiana	Let's Go, Hoosiers!	Aimee Aryal
Iowa	Hello, Herky!	Aimee Aryal
Iowa State	Hello, Cy!	Amy DeLashmutt
James Madison	Hello, Duke Dog!	Aimee Aryal
Kansas	Hello, Big Jay!	Aimee Aryal
Kansas State	Hello, Willie!	Dan Walter
Kentucky	Hello, Wildcat!	Aimee Aryal
LSU	Hello, Mike!	Aimee Aryal
LSU	Mike's Journey Through the Bayou State	Aimee Aryal
Maryland	Hello, Testudo!	Aimee Aryal
Michigan	Let's Go, Blue!	Aimee Aryal
Michigan State	Hello, Sparty!	Aimee Aryal
Minnesota	Hello, Goldy!	Aimee Aryal
Mississippi	Hello, Colonel Rebel!	Aimee Aryal

Pro Football

Carolina Panthers	Let's Go, Panthers!	Aimee Aryal
Chicago Bears	Let's Go, Bears!	Aimee Aryal
Dallas Cowboys	How 'Bout Them Cowboys!	Aimee Aryal
Green Bay Packers	Go, Pack, Go!	Aimee Aryal
Kansas City Chiefs	Let's Go, Chiefs!	Aimee Aryal
Minnesota Vikings	Let's Go, Vikings!	Aimee Aryal
New York Giants	Let's Go, Giants!	Aimee Aryal
New York Jets	J-E-T-S! Jets, Jets, Jets!	Aimee Aryal
New England Patriots	Let's Go, Patriots!	Aimee Aryal
Seattle Seahawks	Let's Go, Seahawks!	Aimee Aryal
Washington Redskins	Hail To The Redskins!	Aimee Aryal

Basketball

Dallas Mavericks	Let's Go, Mavs!	Mark Cuban
Boston Celtics	Let's Go, Celtics!	Aimee Aryal

Other

Kentucky Derby	White Diamond Runs For The Roses	Aimee Aryal
Marine Corps Marathon	Run, Miles, Run!	Aimee Aryal
Mississippi State	Hello, Bully!	Aimee Aryal
Missouri	Hello, Truman!	Todd Donoho
Nebraska	Hello, Herbie Husker!	Aimee Aryal
North Carolina	Hello, Rameses!	Aimee Aryal
North Carolina	Rameses' Journey Through the Tar Heel State	Aimee Aryal
North Carolina St.	Hello, Mr. Wuf!	Aimee Aryal
North Carolina St.	Mr. Wuf's Journey Through North Carolina	Aimee Aryal
Notre Dame	Let's Go, Irish!	Aimee Aryal
Ohio State	Hello, Brutus!	Aimee Aryal
Ohio State	Brutus' Journey	Aimee Aryal
Oklahoma	Let's Go, Sooners!	Aimee Aryal
Oklahoma State	Hello, Pistol Pete!	Aimee Aryal
Oregon	Go Ducks!	Aimee Aryal
Oregon State	Hello, Benny the Beaver!	Aimee Aryal
Penn State	Hello, Nittany Lion!	Aimee Aryal
Penn State	We Are Penn State!	Joe Paterno
Purdue	Hello, Purdue Pete!	Aimee Aryal
Rutgers	Hello, Scarlet Knight!	Aimee Aryal
South Carolina	Hello, Cocky!	Aimee Aryal
South Carolina	Cocky's Journey Through the Palmetto State	Aimee Aryal
So. California	Hello, Tommy Trojan!	Aimee Aryal
Syracuse	Hello, Otto!	Aimee Aryal
Tennessee	Hello, Smokey!	Aimee Aryal
Tennessee	Smokey's Journey Through the Volunteer State	Aimee Aryal
Texas	Hello, Hook 'Em!	Aimee Aryal
Texas	Hook 'Em's Journey Through the Lone Star State	Aimee Aryal
Texas A & M	Howdy, Reveille!	Aimee Aryal
Texas A & M	Reveille's Journey Through the Lone Star State	Aimee Aryal
Texas Tech	Hello, Masked Rider!	Aimee Aryal
UCLA	Hello, Joe Bruin!	Aimee Aryal
Virginia	Hello, CavMan!	Aimee Aryal
Virginia Tech	Hello, Hokie Bird!	Aimee Aryal
Virginia Tech	Yea, It's Hokie Game Day!	Frank Beamer
Virginia Tech	Hokie Bird's Journey Through Virginia	Aimee Aryal
Wake Forest	Hello, Demon Deacon!	Aimee Aryal
Washington	Hello, Harry the Husky!	Aimee Aryal
Washington State	Hello, Butch!	Aimee Aryal
West Virginia	Hello, Mountaineer!	Aimee Aryal
Wisconsin	Hello, Bucky!	Aimee Aryal
Wisconsin	Bucky's Journey Through the Badger State	Aimee Aryal

Order online at **mascotbooks.com** using promo code " **free**" to receive **FREE SHIPPING**!

More great titles coming soon!

info@mascotbooks.com

MASCOT BOOKS

SCHOOL PROGRAM

Promote reading. Build spirit. Raise money.™

Mascot Books® is creating customized children's books for public and private elementary schools all across America. Containing school-specific story lines and illustrations, our books are beloved by principals, librarians, teachers, parents, and of course, by young readers.

Our books feature your mascot taking a tour of your school, while highlighting all the things and events that make your school community such a special place.

The Mascot Books Elementary School Program is an innovative way to promote reading and build spirit, while offering a fresh, new marketing or fundraising opportunity.

Starting Is As Easy As 1-2-3!

1 You tell us all about your school community. What makes your school unique? What are your well-known traditions? Why do parents and students love your school?

2 With the information you share with us, Mascot Books creates a one-of-a-kind hardcover children's book featuring your school and your mascot.

3 Your book is delivered!

Great new fundraising idea for public schools!

Innovative way to market your private school to potential new students!